THIS LITTLE TIGER BOOK BELONGS TO:

_____

_____

_____

_____

D0543134

3 0120 01950541 1

It's my turn!

by David Bedford

illustrated by Elaine Field

ISLINGTON LIBRARIES	
LIBRARY & ACC. No.	LJ.
CLASS No.	F
CATG'D	DATE

Oscar and Tilly found a playground.
"Shall we play on the slide?" asked Oscar.
"I'll go first," said Tilly.

"I'll go now," said Oscar.
"Not yet," said Tilly.
"It's not your turn."

"That looks fun,"
said Oscar.
"Is it my turn now?"
"Not yet," said Tilly.

Tilly went round and round on the roundabout.
"Is it my turn yet?" asked Oscar.
"No," said Tilly. "I haven't finished."

"I feel dizzy,"
said Tilly.

"I feel better now," said Tilly.
"Can I slide after you?"
"No," said Oscar. "It's not your turn."

"Can I go on the swing after you?"
asked Tilly.
"No," said Oscar. "It's still my turn."

"Get off, Tilly," shouted Oscar.
"It's my turn on the see-saw."
"The see-saw doesn't work," said Tilly.
But when Oscar jumped on the other end . . .

Then Tilly
came down
and . . .

Oscar went up . . . .

Oscar and Tilly
played together
all afternoon.

Join the LITTLE TIGER CLUB now for lots more books to enjoy!

Schools can join too and will receive a special enrolment pack.

JOIN THE LITTLE TIGER CLUB

Once you've become a member of the Little Tiger Club, you will receive details of special offers, competitions and news of new books. Why not write a book review? The best review received will be published on book covers or in the Little Tiger Press catalogue.

The LITTLE TIGER CLUB is free to all members who can cancel their membership at any time, and are under no obligation to purchase any books. If you would like details of the Little Tiger Club or a catalogue of books please contact: Little Tiger Press, 1 The Coda Centre, 189 Munster Road, London SW6 6AW, UK.
Telephone: 020 7385 6333 Fax: 020 7385 7333
e-mail info@littletiger.co.uk

For Deborah
~ D.B.
For Maddy
~ E.F.

LITTLE TIGER PRESS
An imprint of Magi Publications
I The Coda Centre, 189 Munster Road, London SW6 6AW
This paperback edition published 2000
First published in Great Britain 2000
Text © 2000 David Bedford
Illustrations © 2000 Elaine Field

David Bedford and Elaine Field have asserted their rights
to be identified as the author and illustrator of this work
under the Copyright, Designs and Patents Act, 1988.

Printed in Belgium by Proost NV, Turnhout
All rights reserved • ISBN I 85430 670 7
3 5 7 9 10 8 6 4 2

LITTLE TIGER PRESS
London